2r

BO, THE FAMOUS RETRIEVER

About The Author

Lynn Sheffield Simmons holds a bachelor's degree in elementary education and a master's degree in special education from Texas Woman's University. She is a member of Phi Delta Kappa honorary fraternity and has taught in the public schools. For many years she has been a freelance writer.

Mrs. Simmons' award-winning column, "Up A Creek," historical reviews, and feature stories have appeared in a number of newspapers and magazines. Her historical pageant, <u>The Place is Argyle</u>, is performed annually in Argyle, Texas. She is also the author of the children's book <u>Sugar Lump, the Orphan Calf</u>.

Mrs. Simmons lives on a small farm in Argyle with her husband, Larry, who has a dental practice in Denton, Texas.

This book is dedicated to my two wonderful mothers:

Mildred B. Nelson
and
Linadine Simmons,

and to my husband, Larry,
for his love and support.

A special thank you to:

Stan Simmons, Terry Lantrip, Oleta North,
Katy Dawson, and Glendine Lipford

Bo, the Famous Retriever
Copyright © 1997

by Lynn Sheffield Simmons

Published by
Argyle Books
710 Old Justin Road
Argyle, Texas 76226

Printed by
Terrill Wheeler Printing, Inc.
Denton, Texas

Illustrations by Lin Hampton

Title Graphics by Stan Simmons

Second Printing, 1998

Printed in the United States of America

Library of Congress
Catalog Card Number: 96-095324

ISBN 0-9642573-1-9

"Hey, slow down!" Drake hollered.

Bo,
THE FAMOUS RETRIEVER

by
Lynn Sheffield Simmons

Printed on Recycled Paper

Contents

Chapter   Page

1   Meeting Bo   1

2   Making New Friends   7

3   The Burglary   16

4   Another New Friend   23

5   Opening Galls   34

6   Gifts for Angels   42

7   Geodes and Rose Rocks   49

8   The Fugitive   54

9   The New Dog Pen   65

10 The Stolen VCR   72

11 A Visit to Henry's Uncle   83

12 Visiting the Detention Center   89

13 The Capture   93

14 The Famous Retriever   103

Chapter 1

Meeting Bo

"I'll be right there," Mrs. Barnett promised, returning the receiver to its cradle and snatching up the local senior citizen's report Pat exclaimed she needed, "Right now. Tonight!"

Since this was Mrs. Barnett's only involvement with a community project, she felt compelled to answer Pat's urgent request. Hurriedly she combed her short, wavy hair and threw a jacket over her shoulders. As she rushed out the door, Bo, her son's eight-month-old Labrador retriever, ran to her with a stick in his mouth. "Not now," she told the black pup, shoving him aside.

He followed her to the car, and as she slid her slender form under the steering wheel, he tried to get in with her. She pushed him aside yelling, "SIT!"

Her son had told her the dog would obey a stern command, but as she drove off Bo followed. She backed the car up to the house, rolled down the window, and shouted, "SIT!"

He did, but only as long as the car wasn't moving. After her third unsuccessful attempt, she decided she was in too much of a hurry to continue this argument. Instead, she ushered him into the house and led him into the kitchen. She gave him a few dog biscuits and then quickly left closing the door behind her.

She reminded herself that Bo was extremely special to her son. He had left on a government job to Alaska two days after he brought the six-month-old pup home, and his parting words were, "Take care of him, Mom. He's going to be a famous retriever."

The dog began to show signs of being a good retriever almost immediately. One morning before she had gotten out of bed, he brought her an uprooted rubber plant from the flower pot in the living room. Then when he ran off with his dog bowl, Mrs. Barnett told him he would have to do without until he brought it back. A couple of hours later, Bo appeared at the door with some child's sand bucket clenched between his teeth.

Now that Bo was confined to the kitchen, Mrs. Barnett left the house. Before traveling very far she realized she needed to turn on her head-lights. Almost instantly, they spotlighted an old, blue pickup truck parked in front of a small rent house on Old Justin Road. Mrs. Barnett noticed a newer black truck parked at the side as she strained to see if she recognized any of the men. Two men were unloading boxes from the old truck while another man was holding open the screen door. Shaking her head, she realized they were not people she had ever seen before.

When she arrived, Pat was waiting for her. Mrs. Barnett's light blonde hair, blended with strands of gray, shined under the porch light as she handed her friend the report.

"Thank you, May," Pat said. "I'm sorry I sounded so urgent, but there is some information in this report I need for my letter to the news-paper."

Pat was accustomed to meeting deadlines for she often wrote letters to the editor on subjects she thought needed the public's attention. Her latest concern was the Argyle Angel Tree. She

Two men were unloading boxes from the old truck while another man was holding open the screen door.

wanted more people to participate by donating gifts to the children who needed them. Anne Crain, who was in charge of the program, was asking residents to take a paper angel from the Christmas tree at the Argyle School. On the back of the angel was a gift number and information about the child. The local senior citizen's organization supported the effort. Mrs. Barnett wrote in her report additional information given to her by Dr. Koonce, the school district's superintendent, and she assumed Pat needed it for her letter.

Handing Pat the report, she assured her that bringing it by had not presented a problem. All at once her thoughts changed to Bo, and it worried her that he might be tearing up the kitchen. Immediately she ended the conversation and left the porch.

Mrs. Barnett's tall, slim frame drifted into the shadows as she rushed to her car. While driving home, she began thinking about the burly looking men she had seen taking boxes into the small rent house. As she passed by, it almost looked deserted except for the black pickup parked at the side and strips of light coming from behind the curtains.

Upon arriving home, she hurried into the house to encounter whatever Bo had chewed up while she was away, but as she inspected the kitchen, surprisingly, she found nothing disturbed.

"He must have slept the whole time," she thought, turning out the kitchen lights before letting Bo outside for a run.

"Maybe he's outgrown his bad behavior," she yawned.

Chapter 2

Making New Friends

In the days that followed, Bo became even better at retrieving. He brought Mrs. Barnett a piece of the door frame he had ripped off the front door, and before she could nail it back, he ran off with the hammer. Later he returned with it clenched between his teeth.

Besides seizing whatever Mrs. Barnett laid down Bo also wanted whatever she held in her hand. One afternoon he attempted to take the newspaper away from her. Grabbing it with his teeth, he tried to jerk it out of her hand, but Mrs. Barnett held on. "No," she commanded sternly, as the black dog pulled harder.

Mrs. Barnett soon became annoyed with his persistence and shoved the paper toward him exclaiming, "If you want it so badly, take it to the house!"

Bo sprang forward with his head held high carrying the newspaper up the driveway. Much to her surprise, he dropped it on the porch and promptly sat down. She picked it up, praised him, and went inside the house. A few seconds later she returned with a dog biscuit and more praises.

Within days Bo had mastered the task and was not only bringing Mrs. Barnett's newspaper to the porch, but everyone else's he could find. Quickly she telephoned her son. "I don't need all of these newspapers," she explained.

"What do you mean it will give me a chance to meet my neighbors? . . . All right, I'll call them."

Her neighbors seemed quite understanding, and they all knew Bo. It surprised her to hear such nice compliments about him. Especially when a few days later, Bo ran to her with a pair of pantyhose hanging out of his mouth. Again she telephoned her son.

"I don't know how long he's been doing things like this. No, I don't think he ripped them off some poor woman — I mean — he ripped off some woman. . . . Oh, I wouldn't dare call. My neighbors are nice enough about their newspapers as long as I return them every evening. Say, I met two new families and . . . What do you mean it's good I'm getting out and broadening my circle of friends? Your dog won't mind me . . . You say, talk to him and speak to him more softly? You mean whisper to him? When are you coming home?"

Shortly after that conversation, she met three pleasantly polite young people getting off the school bus. Bo must have heard the vehicle stop, and having become bored from lying in the sun all afternoon, he probably thought he'd stir up some activity by snatching Mrs. Barnett's sun hat off her head in an attempt to get her to chase him. She yelled for him to sit, but he ignored the command, prancing down the street with his head high and Mrs. Barnett's hat hanging out of his mouth. She shouted at him, and when that didn't work she tried whispering. He continued his mission, marching straight to the children getting off the bus. One boy grabbed the dog and gently held his head as he softly ordered, "Release."

Immediately the dog dropped the hat into his hand. As the boy gave it to Mrs. Barnett, the girl standing beside him asked, "Would you like

He continued his mission, marching straight to the children getting off the bus.

for us to walk the dog back to your house?"

"That would be very kind of you," she sighed, still winded from her chase.

After the youngsters introduced themselves, Mrs. Barnett introduced Bo. The boy named Horace told her, "Bo meets our bus nearly every day with that stick he carries in his mouth, but this is the first time he's met us with a hat."

"Yes, we really like him, but we haven't known what to call him until now," said Drake, the young man who had reclaimed her hat.

When they entered the house, Mrs. Barnett offered them milk and cookies. Amy, the girl with them, passed the napkins and poured the milk. Observing the dog as he wagged his tail watching each one of the guests take a cookie from the plate, Amy asked, "Does Bo get one?"

"No, he has his own treats," Mrs. Barnett answered, giving him a dog biscuit.

"These are good cookies," Amy remarked, taking another bite. "Did you bake them?"

"Yes, I try to keep the cookie jar full and have done so for years. I suppose old habits are hard to change which reminds me, Bo has gotten into a habit I would like to change. He brings home all my neighbors' newspapers. It's about this time of the day that he grabs the newspaper off the lawn, brings it to my door, and then runs to get more before I can stop him. Do you have any suggestions?"

"I guess you could tie him up every after-noon," said Drake, helping himself to another cookie.

"I tried that, but he howls terribly and pulls on his chain so hard I'm afraid he'll hurt his neck. I am tired of returning all those newspapers."

"Does he go with you when you return them?" Amy asked.

"No, I chain him up, and for some reason he doesn't misbehave. He only acts that way when the newspapers are being delivered."

"Do you throw the papers on the lawn?"

"No," she responded. "Most of the time the neighbors are at home, and I hand it to them, but if they aren't I leave it inside the screen door."

"Hey, I know what we can do," said Horace, his dark eyes dancing with excitement. "After he brings your newspaper to the door, we can keep him busy playing fetch and. . . ."

"After a few days he'll forget about getting the other newspapers," interrupted Drake, getting caught up in Horace's scheme.

"And in order to get all that energy you'll need to throw the stick, you'll have to eat some of Mrs. Barnett's homemade cookies," Amy teased, taking another one from the plate.

"That's a splendid idea. I'd rather bake cookies for the three of you than return those newspapers."

Bo began barking and scratching at the door.

"Do you see why I have to LET HIM OUT?" Mrs. Barnett inquired, trying to talk over the dog's loud barks while unlatching the door.

The three of them watched in amazement as Bo snatched the newspaper off the lawn, deposited it on the porch, and ran to a neighboring house.

"Where's that stick you were going to throw him?" Amy quipped.

"He didn't give us a chance to get outside," Horace replied, disbelieving the dog's swiftness.

"Drake, tomorrow we're going to put him on a leash BEFORE he gets out the door."

They continued to watch Bo run from house to house returning each time to deposit a newspaper. When he finished, he showed signs of being completely exhausted, dropping to the steps. Mrs. Barnett grabbed his collar and led him to the new dog house she had bought him. After hooking him to the chain mounted on the side, she proceeded to deliver the newspapers to her neighbors as the three young people helped. Upon returning home she telephoned her son to tell him about her interesting afternoon.

"I think I have my afternoon paper route solved. . . . No, they aren't going to return them. They're going to keep Bo busy after he delivers mine. . . . How did you know they liked the cookies? . . . Well, your generation did, but these youngsters might have different tastes. . . . Kay Clark called and asked if you wanted Bo's sister. I told her one was enough. . . . Yes, I bragged on him. I told her he was healthy. What? . . .If you want him to learn how to shake hands, you come teach him yourself. . . .We'll talk later."

Hanging up the receiver, she grabbed the

newspaper. "Pat's letter to the editor should be in here by now," she thought, turning to the editorial page.

"There it was, 'Angel Tree in Need of Gifts,'" she read to herself.

It surprised her that people taking an angel from the tree could drop their presents off not only at the school, but at the Argyle City Hall and Johnny Joe's convenience store as well.

"That's a new piece of information," she thought. When she folded the newspaper, she noticed the date.

"My goodness," she reflected, "this was yesterday's paper."

Chapter 3

The Burglary

The next afternoon Bo ran to meet the school bus while Mrs. Barnett stood on the lawn. As he brought the three young people up the drive, Amy ran ahead.

"Did you hear about the burglary?"

"No, where?"

"Right here on Old Justin Road," blurted Drake.

"Come in for some apple juice and oatmeal cookies while you tell me all about it."

They sat around the kitchen table as the three of them took turns adding bits of information surrounding the burglary that had happened the day before only a few houses away.

"Chief Partin thinks it might be someone

who knows the habits of the neighborhood because Mrs. Hill is nearly always at home except on the days she's called to do substitute teaching, and the Argyle school called her yesterday morning," Horace said.

"I bet she no sooner dropped her kids off at her mother's house than the burglars were there," said Drake, reaching for a cookie as he continued to speak. "They took a VCR, camcorder, television, some cameras, all Mrs. Hill's jewelry, and the afternoon newspaper."

Mrs. Barnett's visitors looked at Bo stretched out on the floor peacefully snoozing. "Oh, he couldn't have," Mrs. Barnett defended, reading her visitors' thoughts. "He hasn't brought anything home lately except newspapers."

"No," Horace said, shaking his head. "He couldn't have carried the television. . . ."

"Or the VCR," interrupted Drake.

"You're lucky to have Bo," said Amy. "I don't think anyone would bother your house."

"Well, if that's true, it's the only thing he's good for because he's surely on my list today."

All of them looked at the satiny, black animal lying contentedly on the floor.

"What could this sweet dog possibly do wrong?" Amy cooed, leaning over to stroke the dog's ear that had fallen across his face.

"Did you notice there is only one barstool at the counter today?"

"Where is the other one?" Drake asked.

"He ate it," Mrs. Barnett answered.

"He must like vinyl," said Amy, quickly defending the dog as she forced herself to keep a straight face, "because vinyl covers the foam rubber padding . . . and . . . you could get it recovered!"

"He likes foam rubber."

"My dog always liked shoes," Horace interjected.

"He likes them too. They were sitting on the barstool."

"He must have thought they were rawhide chewies," said Drake, trying not to smile.

"They were still in the box."

"Bo! You awful dog!" Amy exclaimed,

pushing her long, blonde hair over her shoulder as she bent over to look at the dog who sleepily opened one eye.

"What happened?" Drake asked.

"After shopping this morning, I came into the house with an armload of packages, and apparently Bo ran in behind me. I put the box with the new pair of shoes in it on the barstool before going outside to fill his water bowl. Then I remembered I needed to put newspapers in the recycling bin. I returned to find the kitchen floor covered with pieces of barstool, bits of cardboard from the shoe box, and Bo," she pointed, "was over there in the corner polishing off the shoes."

"He must be fast!" Drake exclaimed.

"Yeah, at polishing off shoes," Horace snickered.

Abruptly, Bo perked up his ears and quickly charged forward. He must have been groggy from his afternoon nap for he clumsily slid across the kitchen floor, attempting to get to the door.

"The newspaper must be here," Mrs. Barnett announced.

"Do you have a leash!" Drake shouted, holding on to the dog's collar.

"Yes," she answered taking it from the peg in the laundry room and handing it to him.

"All right, Horace, open the door, and I'll walk him on his leash."

When Horace opened the door, Bo bolted out dragging Drake with him.

"Hey, slow down!" Drake hollered, holding on to the leash with both hands and planting his feet firmly on the ground.

Bo continued his speed, taking large leaps forward. Swiftly, the dog snatched up the newspaper, deposited it on the porch, and bounded across the lawn pulling Drake behind. "WHOOOAA, BO!" Drake yelled as he slid across the grass.

Horace jumped in front of them, but the black dog ran around him.

"Let go!" screeched Amy as Drake began to run as fast as he could to keep up with the dog. They were returning from the house next door when Drake's foot hit a rock causing him to drop the leash and stumble across the lawn, almost falling, but catching his balance before plummeting to the ground. Collapsing on the porch, Drake tried catching his breath. "That . . . dog . . . is strong," he wheezed.

"I bet your arms are two inches longer," laughed Horace.

"You . . . try . . . it . . . next time."

They watched as the black dog continued running to the houses, snatching up newspapers, and dropping them on the porch.

"I don't think we can break him of this," Mrs. Barnett said.

"I don't think I want to try," Drake sighed, shaking his head.

"All right, let's chain him up and return the newspapers," Mrs. Barnett suggested.

After the deliveries, Mrs. Barnett let Bo off his chain when she noticed the side of his dog house. "I can't believe it! That was brand new!" she exclaimed.

"You are a bad dog," she declared, shaking her finger at him as he patiently sat there and listened. "You've chewed a hole in the side of your dog house. How did you do that? Well, you'll just have to live with it."

Irritated by Bo's latest misdeed, Mrs. Barnett marched through the front door leaving him outside.

Chapter 4

Another New Friend

The next afternoon, Bo brought to the door not only Mrs. Barnett's three new friends, but a fourth person. His name was Henry Green. This was his first day of school since arriving to Texas from Oklahoma. He told them he was living on Old Justin Road. "I didn't know we had any houses for sale on this street," said Mrs. Barnett.

"We didn't buy," Henry told her, helping himself to a cookie as the plate passed his way. "My uncle and I are renting."

"Oh yes," Mrs. Barnett acknowledged, "the house across from the county barn."

At the same time they learned that Henry was a year older than the other three, although he was in the same grade.

"My Uncle Jimmy and I have done a lot of

traveling for the past two years, and I keep getting behind in school," he had said.

They also learned his parents were killed in
an automobile accident two years before, and his
Uncle Jimmy, whom Henry hadn't known very
well, was now his guardian.

"My parents left everything to me, but it's
in a trust fund that my uncle is in charge of until
I am eighteen," he divulged.

"We are glad you moved here, Henry. Did
Horace and Drake tell you about their experience
with Bo yesterday?" Mrs. Barnett asked.

"No, but Amy did."

"I couldn't help it," she giggled, "Bo was
pulling Drake as if he was grass skiing."

They all laughed, including Drake. "Well,
what are we going to try today?" Mrs. Barnett
inquired.

"I think we ought to let him retrieve the
newspapers and all of us deliver them back to
where they belong," suggested Drake.

"I agree," Mrs. Barnett said, watching Bo
as he jumped up and ran to the door, barking.

She opened the door to let him out as the four guests watched. "Look how he runs!" Amy squealed, excitedly.

"You ought to be on the other end," Drake laughed.

"I'm glad you're able to laugh about it," Mrs. Barnett said, complimenting Drake on his attitude.

After Bo brought the newspapers to Mrs. Barnett's porch, he dropped down beside them. They let him rest awhile before escorting him to his dog house. Drake put Bo on his chain. It was then Horace noticed the side of the dog house, "Where did that hole come from?"

"His teeth," Mrs. Barnett sighed. "He chewed it yesterday."

"Bo, you get into all sorts of trouble," said Amy, addressing the dog.

"Let's deliver the papers. Henry, what time does your uncle get home from work?" Mrs. Barnett asked.

"He isn't working right now. He and some of his friends are making plans to start a new business though."

"They must have been the rather large men I saw taking boxes into your house the other evening," Mrs. Barnett said.

"Yes, they were helping us move stuff in."

"What kind of business are they going into?" Amy inquired.

"I don't know. They're always planning something. Hey, if you have any of those newspapers left, I'd like to have one. We haven't started taking one yet, and I'd like to read more about the Angel Tree."

"We probably won't have any left," smiled Mrs. Barnett, puzzled that Henry knew about the Angel Tree.

"What are these round balls lying on the ground?" Drake inquired.

"I don't know," Horace answered, examining the small, brown sphere he picked up off the ground, "but they are all around here."

"When you come tomorrow, I'll show you," Mrs. Barnett informed them.

The teenagers went home after making the deliveries, and Mrs. Barnett let Bo off his chain.

It didn't look as if he had chewed any more of his dog house, making her feel a little more friendly toward him, and so she let him in the house. She was clearing her supper dishes off the table when the telephone rang.

It was Vandi Brown, chairperson of the Argyle Pride Task Force, asking Mrs. Barnett to help design a walking and jogging path around a portion of the school. Mrs. Barnett's neighbors had told Vandi she liked to walk. This was the excuse Mrs. Barnett had used when telling her neighbors she would return their newspapers after some had asked if they could pick them up.

"Oh, no," she had said, "I wouldn't hear of your coming by. Besides, I like to walk."

Vandi asked Mrs. Barnett if she had heard about the burglary.

"Yes," she answered.

Vandi lived off Skyline Drive, a neighborhood close to Old Justin Road.

"Do you live far from where it took place?" she asked.

"No, I don't," Mrs. Barnett answered, "and I think this should make everyone more careful about locking their doors."

"I understand you have a good size dog," Vandi replied. "He must be a lot of comfort to you."

Not wanting to discuss Bo, Mrs. Barnett quickly changed the subject back to the meeting scheduled the next day at city hall. Then she ended their conversation with the promise, "I'll be there tomorrow."

The following morning when she arrived at city hall, she remembered she had left her notes in the car. Quickly she turned around to go back through the door when she almost collided into Police Chief Larry Partin, who was entering the building. Mrs. Barnett instantly recognized him because they had talked recently when he pulled alongside her as she walked home from delivering the newspapers.

"Nice evening to take a walk, isn't it Mrs. Barnett?" he had asked, slowing down his vehicle to roll alongside.

"Yes, it is," she agreed, not wanting to discuss her ridiculous reason for walking.

"If you ever need anything, be sure to give

us a call," he volunteered in a nice, friendly voice before driving off.

Now he quickly stepped aside to avoid a collision as Mrs. Barnett laughed, "Are you in a hurry, or am I going the wrong way?"

"Neither one," he smiled. "What can I do for you?"

"I'm here for a meeting, but while I have you here I would like to ask you about the burglary on Old Justin Road. Were you able to find any clues as to who did it?"

"The sheriff's department lifted a thumb print from the door frame of the Hill's house, and I sent it to AFIS for identification," he said.

"What's AFIS?"

"Automated Fingerprint Identifying System," he answered. "It is a system developed by the FBI where they can match any fingerprint with the computer."

"But what if the person doesn't have his fingerprints on file?"

"Nearly everyone has been fingerprinted at one time or another. I would imagine they have yours."

"Now, Chief Partin, I have never gone to jail," she answered, acting a little offended.

"I didn't mean to imply that," he quickly responded. "If you have ever had a passport, visa, or been in the military service you have had your fingerprints taken, and now they take them when you get your driver's license."

"That's right. I have been fingerprinted," she nodded. "My husband was in the military, and we lived overseas a few years. This is so interesting. Let me know what you find out."

At the meeting, Vandi explained that the City had formed the Argyle Pride Task Force for members to set up a beautification program. City officials wanted to improve the city's appearance and encourage residents to take more pride in their homes. The money to pay for the projects would come from the organization's fund-raising activities.

"We have enough money for Pride Day Clean-Up," Vandi continued. "The task force rented three large, trash dumpsters to be delivered to the school's parking lot Saturday morning for residents to dispose of unwanted furniture or refuse."

Mrs. Barnett and a few others volunteered to be at the parking lot during the day to set aside any discarded items suitable for the garage sale they planned to have later. Before the meeting adjourned, they discussed the bake sale scheduled at the same time as the clean-up. Mrs. Barnett offered to bake six dozen oatmeal cookies and said she would be at the school early Saturday morning.

Upon arriving home, Mrs. Barnett let Bo off his chain for a run. Then she sat down to have a cup of tea. After she finished, she looked out the window and noticed the black dog lying on the porch, instead of pawing at the door as usual.

"Are you sick?" she asked, letting him inside.

In a flash she grabbed his collar and yelled, "No, No! Outside!"

Pulling him out the door with one hand and holding her nose with the other she exclaimed, "You stay out here until that awful smell blows off of you!"

Re-entering the house, she promptly grabbed the telephone. "This is your mother, and your dog has been playing with skunks. . . . What do you mean give him a bath? I can't stand to get close to him. . . . Yes, I have some tomato juice. Do I pour it on him or in him? . . . Let's hang up, and I'll give it a try."

Hurriedly she snatched a bottle of tomato juice off the pantry shelf. Then she went into the bathroom for a towel, shampoo, and a pair of rubber gloves. She took her gatherings to the outside hose and called Bo. Slowly he walked to her with his head drooping and his tail curled between his legs, not looking at all well.

"I'd be sick, too, if I smelled as bad as you do," she said, pouring the tomato juice over his back while keeping her head turned in the opposite direction.

The dog stood patiently as she covered his body. "This is supposed to make you smell better," she informed him, "so we'll leave it on for a while before washing it off."

While they waited, she gently patted the docile animal. After she shampooed him with a sweet-smelling soap, she bent over the faucet to turn off the water. Bo began shaking himself, spraying Mrs. Barnett.

"Stop that!" she scolded, wiping her face with one hand and throwing a towel over his back with the other.

Bo started running in circles. Picking up the towel, Mrs. Barnett ran after him.

"Sit, Bo!" she yelled. He raced past her, tucking his tail and running in tight circles around her legs. She turned with him, grabbing for him now and then as she waved the towel.

In a flash, Bo flipped on his back, scooting and wiggling across the grass. Mrs. Barnett threw herself across him. Seizing one leg, she held on until he quit twisting and turning. Then she began rubbing him with the towel, sniffing his coat occasionally. "I guess you smell nice enough to come into the house," she affirmed, getting up off the ground and leading him to the porch.

Chapter 5

Opening Galls

That afternoon when the four youths got off the school bus, Bo met them with a stick in his mouth. Henry played fetch with him by throwing the stick high in the air and yelling, "Fetch!" The black dog grabbed it the instant it hit the ground and returned it to him.

"Say, he's getting pretty good at bringing that back to you. He'll bring it back to Horace and me the first few times, but after that he takes it off somewhere," commented Drake as Henry threw it again.

"I really like playing with him," Henry said, stroking the dog's head after he returned.

Mrs. Barnett met them at the door, inviting them into the kitchen for juice and cookies.

"Did you notice how nice and clean Bo is?"

Mrs. Barnett asked.

"He surely is," said Amy, rubbing the dog's satiny coat. "Did you give him a bath?"

"Well, it started out that way, but I ended up getting one too."

Mrs. Barnett told them about Bo's foul odor that resembled the smell of, "more than one skunk."

"Did a whole family of black and white kitty cats spray you, Bo?" Amy grinned, petting the dog.

"I would like to have seen you give him a bath," Henry laughed, as he pictured Mrs. Barnett chasing Bo.

"It wasn't a very pretty sight," she said, shaking her head.

While they were sitting at the table drinking Mrs. Barnett's fruit punch and eating her peanut butter cookies, Horace asked her to tell them about the little, brown balls they found.

"Do you have any with you?"

"Sure," he replied, standing up to pull them out of his pocket.

Mrs. Barnett left the table returning a few seconds later with a small knife, a block of wood, and a newspaper. "To keep from cutting the table and making a mess, we will put this newspaper over the block of wood. Do you have any idea what this might be?" she asked, holding up the little, brown ball.

"Something like an acorn?" Horace questioned.

"No, but it did come off an oak tree," she answered.

"If it were a rock, my uncle would probably try to sell it," Henry grinned, taking the round ball and turning it over. "Hey, this does look like some of his rocks."

"He's selling rocks?" Amy asked.

Before Henry could answer, Mrs. Barnett informed them it was not a rock and asked her guests what they expected to find when she cut it open.

"Something like the inside of a nut," declared Horace.

"No, I think it's just air," Amy threw in.

"Amy, if it was just air you could squeeze it or mash it, but this is too hard to crush," Henry determined.

"You are right. They are very sturdy," said Mrs. Barnett, taking the ball from Henry and holding it tightly on the newspaper as she began cutting it with the knife. "This is called a gall, and it's hard to cut. That's why I have to saw back and forth." A brown colored dust scattered on the newspaper as she continued cutting.

"What's that powder stuff?" Amy asked, petting Bo after he walked over to sit beside her.

"It's tannin," she explained as she continued her cutting, "and it is sometimes used for dyeing or to make ink."

"How do you know all of this?" Drake asked.

"I used to teach eighth grade science," she divulged.

"I thought so," he confirmed, folding his arms over his chest and nodding.

"Oh, you did not," Amy chided.

"Yes, I did," Drake answered back, placing his hands on the table and leaning forward. "I could tell by the way she talks."

"When I get to the middle of this, you'll be surprised at what we'll find," Mrs. Barnett continued. "An insect has laid eggs in the bark of an oak tree, and in order to protect itself, the oak tree has grown this gall around it. Therefore, the tree isn't invaded by the insects, and the eggs are in a protective cocoon."

When she reached the middle of the gall, there was an indention in the center that held a small white larva.

"Ooooh, a worm," Amy shivered, looking at the translucent larva.

"What kind of an insect is it?" Horace asked, hovering over it.

"A gall fly," she informed them. "Once my science class opened one and found a small fly. I'm sure your next question will be: how does it get out? I assume it eats its way out because often I have found some with nothing in them but a small hole leading to the outside."

"Can we open another one?" Horace asked. "This is really neat."

Before cutting into the next one, Bo jumped up and ran to the door.

"Newspaper time!" Drake shouted, running to let Bo outside.

"Let him do his newspaper snatching while we finish cutting this gall," Mrs. Barnett suggested as her guests nodded in agreement.

The next gall had a number of small larvae wiggling inside.

"I wonder if they would be good for fishing?" Horace asked.

"I don't know, but if you found one large enough to put on a hook, it might be," Mrs. Barnett acknowledged.

"Let's find some more," said Henry.

"We can when we return the newspapers," Mrs. Barnett advised, carefully folding the paper she had used for the cuttings. "I imagine Bo has completed his task by now."

They went outside and sure enough Bo was lying on the porch beside a stack of newspapers. They began making their deliveries after chaining Bo to his dog house.

"Henry, did I hear you say your uncle was now selling rocks?" Mrs. Barnett asked.

"Well, it's his new get-rich-quick idea," Henry began. "As I told you, he and his buddies are always looking for a quick way to make money. When we were in Arkansas last year, we met a man who told us a person could make a lot of money selling rocks, the kind that have animals and plants in them."

"Oh, you're talking about fossils," replied Mrs. Barnett.

"Yes, ma'am," he agreed, "and this man said he paid for a trip all the way across the United States by selling and trading rocks - I mean fossils."

"Does your uncle have very many?" Amy inquired.

"He sure does — boxes full."

"And they are all fossils?" Amy asked.

"No, he has a bunch of other kind too. Some of them are real pretty. I'll bring a few of the small ones tomorrow."

"Ouch!" Horace yelled, dropping the galls and shaking his hand.

"Fire ants!" Mrs. Barnett exclaimed, rushing to him. "You better come with me, and let me take care of your hand."

"Wait for us," she told the others. "We'll be back in a minute."

"I think these critters were put here to cause pain," Horace declared, rubbing his hand as they entered Mrs. Barnett's kitchen.

"It might be, but we don't always know," she confessed, washing Horace's hand and dabbing the stings with ammonia.

"Believe me. It's to cause pain," he affirmed, as Mrs. Barnett topped the stings with a paste of water and baking soda. Then they returned to the others to make their deliveries.

"I'm sorry I won't be home tomorrow," Mrs. Barnett apologized. "It's Saturday, and my friend, Martha, and I are going to Dallas to do some shopping. I'll be home Monday afternoon when you get out of school. Would you like to come then?"

"Sure," they agreed. Everyone left going their separate ways.

Chapter 6

Gifts for Angels

The next morning when Martha pulled her car in the driveway, she watched Mrs. Barnett lead Bo to his dog house. Bowls of fresh water sat on each side. Earlier that morning as Mrs. Barnett placed the bowls beside his house she reasoned, "If he knocks one over, he'll have the other one."

"We need to stop by the school first," Martha called to Mrs. Barnett who was walking to the car after securing Bo to his dog house.

"I need to pick up an angel from the Angel Tree," she continued as Mrs. Barnett climbed into the car.

"I need to get one too." she sighed, smoothing her dress before buckling the seat belt.

Martha parked the car in front of the administration building, and both ladies got out. While they were in the foyer looking at the Christmas tree that held the paper angels, Dr. Koonce entered the building. After he greeted them, Martha asked, "Is there a school board meeting this morning?"

"No, Chief Partin wants to meet with me. What are you ladies doing today?"

"We are going to Dallas to visit Martha's mother and to do some shopping," replied Mrs. Barnett, secretly wondering if they were meeting to discuss the burglary at the Hill's house.

"Yes," Martha added. "Even though it is late fall, the holidays will be here before you know it."

"I'm glad to see you are taking an angel from the tree," he said. "We still have a lot left."

"Has the only publicity been the letter to the editor?" Mrs. Barnett inquired.

"That's all I've seen," said Martha with Dr. Koonce nodding in agreement.

"I'll ask the editor of our weekly newspaper, <u>The Argyle Sun</u>, if he will write a story," Mrs. Barnett volunteered.

The women said goodbye and left for Dallas.

"Do you remember what day Pat's letter was in the newspaper?" Mrs. Barnett asked.

"Yes, Monday afternoon," she answered.

"The afternoon before the burglary at the Hill's house," Mrs. Barnett said out loud.

"What made you think of that?" her friend asked.

"I thought it was curious that the burglars took the newspaper that happened to have Pat's letter in it."

"It's such a shame we are having any kind of crime in Argyle, but I see you have a new dog to protect you. Tell me about him," Martha urged, leaving the service road to enter the interstate.

"He's not mine," she said emphatically. "He's my son's, and I'm just keeping the dog while he's in Alaska. Bo's made so many changes in my life I'm not sure I want to talk about him."

By the time they reached their destination, however, Mrs. Barnett had told her all about Bo, not withholding one detail. "Because of delivering those newspapers every evening my neighbors think I'm some kind of a health nut. Can you imagine?"

"Maybe these are positive changes in your life," suggested Martha.

"Some are, but Bo tearing up everything isn't."

"I'm sure he'll outgrow that. In fact, he probably already has," she smiled.

They had lunch with Martha's mother. Then the two women shopped in department stores for personal needs and presents for the Argyle Angel Tree.

Mrs. Barnett picked out a pair of jeans in size 6, a blue plaid shirt, and two pairs of socks for the five-year-old boy's descriptions she had gotten from the tree.

"Now to find a suitable toy and I will have this lad fixed up," Mrs. Barnett said to Martha who was engaged in selecting hair ribbons for an eight-year-old girl.

Looking through the toy department, both women were undecided on what to buy. "I think little boys still like cars and trucks," Mrs. Barnett said, picking out a small fire truck and a police car while Martha settled on a Barbie doll.

Returning home they turned into Mrs. Barnett's driveway. Both women were shocked by what they saw. Covering Mrs. Barnett's lawn were bits and pieces of wood — a portion of the roof here, a part there, a piece of door frame here, and a section of the dog house there. Chewed and broken fragments littered the drive. Mrs. Barnett left the car stunned. Out of the blue, Bo came running across the lawn carrying a newspaper and dragging a chain still attached to part of the dog house.

Mrs. Barnett didn't take the time to put down her packages before she began dialing the telephone.

"Yes, I know you are at work. That's the number I dialed. Your dog has torn up his dog house and scattered it all over the yard. Martha couldn't even get up the drive. . . . What do you mean, get the kids to help me pick it up? This is Saturday, which reminds me, why are you working on Saturday? . . . That's too technical for me, but I guess it's a good reason. When are you coming home? . . . You say enroll him in a

Both women were shocked by what they saw.

kindergarten. Son, I don't know any teacher who would have him. . . . Oh, a doggie class. That won't help me now. I'll talk to you later."

Over the weekend Mrs. Barnett cleaned up the yard and delivered newspapers.

Chapter 7

Geodes and Rose Rocks

Monday afternoon when the young people got off the school bus, Mrs. Barnett didn't hesitate to tell them about her latest crisis.

"He must have strong teeth," voiced Horace.

"This dog," she said, looking down at his black, satiny form lying at her feet, "has strong teeth, strong jaws, and a strong will."

"He was going to get those newspapers no matter what," said Drake.

"Even if he had to drag the dog house with him," laughed Amy.

"And when it held him back, he ate it," Mrs. Barnett filled in. "Henry, did you bring some rocks?"

"Yes, I did," he responded, taking them out his jacket pocket.

Drake immediately chose one, "Hey, you're right. This does look like a gall."

"Those are geodes," Mrs. Barnett informed them. "Some are hollow inside, and some have crystals."

"How can you tell which ones have crystals?" Horace inquired.

"After you break them open," she disclosed.

"Let's open them," Henry suggested.

"All right," said Mrs. Barnett, taking a newspaper, block of wood, hammer, and knife out of the closet and bringing them to the table. "I brought everything we need to open the galls you picked up Friday and to open the geodes."

They took turns cutting open the galls. Each of them found a small white larva, but none large enough to put on a fish hook.

"I'll get a paper sack for us to break open the geode," Mrs. Barnett volunteered.

Putting the geode inside, she handed it to Henry. "Place the sack on the block of wood, and gently hit it with the hammer."

After Henry tapped the bulge in the sack,

the geode broke instantly. Carefully he pulled out the glittering pieces.

"These are so pretty," said Amy, amazed at their sparkle.

"I have an arrowhead, and it's made out of a rock." Henry passed the pointed arrow to Horace. "I also have a smoked quartz crystal from Arkansas and a rose rock from Oklahoma that . . ."

Bo interrupted Henry by barking and running to the door.

"Paper time!" Amy shouted.

Drake let the dog outside and came back to the table.

Mrs. Barnett picked up the rose rock, "This can be cleaned with a dental pick to look exactly like a rose. The Oklahoma legislature made it the official state rock about thirty years ago. Are you familiar with the legend?"

The four of them shook their heads.

"It's a Cherokee Indian legend. In the 1800's our government had the Cherokees leave their homelands on the east coast to make new homes in the 'Indian territory,' which is now the state of Oklahoma. While the Indians were on this journey, the 'Trail of Tears,' they suffered many hardships and thousands died. In Indian folklore, the story is told that God looked down from heaven. Seeing all the heartache and pain, He memorialized each maiden's tear and each brave's drop of blood that fell to the ground by turning it into the shape of this Cherokee Rose. It's a flower that grew in the Indians' eastern home-land. According to the story, the rocks are abun-dant in Oklahoma because it marks the end of the 'Trail of Tears.'"

"That's a sad story," Amy lamented, look-ing at the rock and turning it over in her hand.

"Indeed it is," Mrs. Barnett agreed, gather-ing up the papers they had used. "We better check on Bo."

Stepping outside, they saw only one news-paper on the porch.

"He's had time to collect more than this," Drake announced, picking it up.

They were waiting for the dog to return, when Horace said, "Something's wrong. That dog should have been back by now. Let's go look for him."

Mrs. Barnett waited for them on the porch. Soon the teenagers returned with Bo running alongside. Amy sprinted ahead.

"You won't believe this, but Mrs. Durham's cat had Bo cornered."

"Yeah," said Drake, catching up with her, "that cat had him hiding under the bushes, and he wouldn't come out until Amy shooed it away."

"Bo," Henry laughed, looking down at the dog, "did you think that kitty would spray you as those skunks did?"

Chapter 8

The Fugitive

Early the next morning Mrs. Barnett answered a knock at the door. It startled her to see a woman dressed in a Denton County Sheriff's Department uniform standing on her porch at 6:30 in the morning. "What has Bo done now?" she thought.

"Ma'am, I don't mean to alarm you, but we are looking for a fugitive who is possibly in the woods behind your house. If you don't have to leave, stay inside, and keep your doors locked," she cautioned.

"Oh, my goodness," murmured Mrs. Barnett, finding it hard to believe her peaceful neighborhood was the center of a manhunt.

Knowing that Argyle did not have a jail, Mrs. Barnett asked where the fugitive came from.

The woman told her that sheriff deputies were answering a call at a rest stop on Interstate-35W between Argyle and Fort Worth when they saw a man sleeping in a truck not having license plates. The deputies awakened him to inquire about the missing truck tags, when he started the engine and took off, nearly hitting two officers. They chased him until he wrecked the truck on John Payne Road and then fled on foot to an area not far from the dense woods behind Mrs. Barnett's house.

Before leaving, the deputy asked Mrs. Barnett to alert her neighbors of the situation and warn them to stay inside their houses with their doors locked.

"I will," Mrs. Barnett promised and then thanked the deputy for stopping by.

Quickly she closed the door, locked it, and hurried to the telephone. "Hello, Kirk, I have some unsettling news," she began as she proceeded to tell her next door neighbor, Kirk Hallum, about the fugitive. During the conversation Kirk offered to contact the neighbors living west of him, which was a relief to Mrs. Barnett because she was unsure of their names. She thanked him and promised to call if she heard any new information. Then she dialed her neighbor living on the east side.

"Oh, my," Donna gasped. "What awful news! I thought you were calling to tell me my cat had your dog trapped under the bushes again."

"No, but it would serve him right for taking your newspapers," Mrs. Barnett responded.

Next, she talked to Nita Grayson, who lived down the street, and asked her to get in touch with her neighbors.

Soon afterward she tried contacting a few more neighbors, not finding many at home. One woman was though, and after telling her about the fugitive, she exclaimed, "So that's why I've been hearing all those sirens!"

"Yes, and you not only need to keep your doors locked, but lock your car as well."

"Not me. I'm going to open the car doors and have the engine running. I want him out of here!"

They both agreed that wouldn't be a good idea and expressed their confidence in the law enforcement officers finding the man soon. The loud whir of a helicopter forced them to end their conversation. Mrs. Barnett had no sooner replaced the receiver than the telephone rang.

It was Donna. "You have a helicopter flying over your house!"

"I KNOW!" Mrs. Barnett screamed into the receiver, "HAVE YOU HEARD ANY NEWS?"

"No, but I'll call when I do!"

With Bo following, Mrs. Barnett darted from one window to another, trying to see — anything. There was nothing but the shadow of a helicopter flying overhead.

The next few telephone calls were from Mrs. Teer, Drake's mother, and Mrs. Beaudine, Amy's mother, both asking if they could bring her anything from the grocery store. She thanked them, saying she had all that she needed for now.

Jack Dalton, a teacher who lived across the street, called from work to tell her how secure the neighborhood was.

"On my way to school this morning sheriff deputies searched my car at a road block on Old Justin and Taylor Roads and then again, at Crawford Road," he said.

She told him she appreciated his call and had barely put down the receiver when Horace's mother called. Mrs. Glass thanked her for treating Horace's fire ant stings and offered to drop him off after school if she needed some company.

"How nice of you to think of me," Mrs. Barnett responded, "but I am fine. Tell Horace that Bo is right here with me."

Mrs. Barnett looked down at the black figure curled up at her feet. "It is comforting to have

"You have a helicopter flying over your house!"

some companionship during a time such as this," she reflected.

"Goodness me, this fugitive business must have me upset," she scolded herself, remembering. "I didn't even correct Donna when she called Bo 'my dog.'"

There was a knock at the door. Both of them jumped. Bo barked as Mrs. Barnett called out, "Who is it?"

"Bobby Anderson," answered a voice from the other side of the door. "Chief Partin thought you might want a visitor for a while."

Mrs. Barnett had known Bobby for years and although she had not seen him recently, she was quite familiar with his voice.

"What a nice surprise," she beamed, opening the door to invite him in. "Sit down, and I'll put on a pot of coffee."

"That sounds good," he grinned, "and if you have any of those cookies, I'll have one of them."

"You know I do," she laughed, remembering all the cookies she had served Bobby and the other volunteers who had attended meetings at her house to plan fund-raising activities for the Argyle Volunteer Fire Department.

All at once the whir of a helicopter grew louder.

"You don't suppose he's in the back yard!" she shrieked, rushing to a back window.

Bobby left the table to look also.

"No, I don't see anything." he said. "You make the coffee. I'll keep looking out back."

Bo sat down beside him, and Bobby reached over to pet the dog as he continued to stare out the window. "You have a good dog here."

"Well, if he is, it just happened today," she said.

"He must know something's going on," Bobby offered, taking his seat back at the table as Bo followed.

Mrs. Barnett set coffee mugs on the table, along with a plate of oatmeal cookies. Then she went to the pantry to get Bo a dog biscuit. She was pouring their coffee when the telephone rang. Kirk was on the other end suggesting they lock up their houses and leave. The helicopter flying overhead almost drowned out their conversation.

"I think we are fine here," Mrs. Barnett assured him. "Bobby Anderson just told me the TEXAS DEPARTMENT OF CORRECTIONS HAS BROUGHT IN SEARCH DOGS, and they are combing the woods. Also, THIS HELICOPTER ISN'T GOING TO LET ANYTHING GET BY IT!" she screamed into the telephone.

"I GUESS YOU'RE RIGHT!" Kirk shouted back.

Bobby and Mrs. Barnett ate cookies and drank coffee, as they laughed about the experiences they shared during their fund raising days for the fire department. Periodically, the telephone would ring, and when Mrs. Barnett answered it, Bobby, with Bo following, would peer out the windows around the house.

One caller was a reporter from the <u>Denton Record-Chronicle</u> covering the manhunt. He had obtained her name from Donna Fielder, a columnist with that newspaper and a friend of Mrs. Barnett's.

"YES!" Mrs. Barnett shouted into the telephone, "THAT IS A HELICOPTER flying over my house."

During their conversation she told him how her neighbors stayed in contact with each other and kept one another informed of the latest developments. Before saying goodbye she asked, "What is this man wanted for?"

Bobby looked puzzled as she listened and sometimes muttered, "Oh, my."

Slowly she put down the receiver. "I'm not so sure I wanted to hear that."

"What's he done?" Bobby asked.

"The man is a murder suspect who is wanted by the Harris County Sheriff's Department. They've been looking for him for the past two weeks. Before this charge, he had been charged with burglary and theft. The authorities consider him quite athletic, and he's known to have survival skills."

"All that, right here in Argyle," Bobby stated, shaking his head.

"Yes, and maybe right out there in the woods," she pointed. Both of them noticed her finger shaking.

"Let's talk about the year we had the barbecue, and no one remembered to take the meat out of the freezer," Bobby laughed. "I never saw so many flustered . . ."

The telephone rang before he could finish. It was Kirk calling to tell her he had checked with the police department only minutes before, and the fugitive was now in custody.

"The search dogs had an easy time flushing him out after the fire ants got him," Kirk chuckled.

Bobby said goodbye and Mrs. Barnett grabbed for the telephone.

"We had that criminal right here, not far from the house," she told her son. "Yes, Bo stayed beside me, and he was as good as gold. . . . I don't think it sounds as if I want him. He's your dog. . . . Oh, yes, they have the fugitive. Everything is calm. The police have left, the road blocks are lifted, and the helicopter is gone. . . . I'll send you a clipping from the afternoon newspaper. . . . OOPS, it just hit the driveway. I've got to let Bo outside. Bye."

Chapter 9

The New Dog Pen

The next afternoon when the teenagers ran up the drive, they saw Mrs. Barnett standing on the porch.

"Did the police find the fugitive close by?" Horace asked as Mrs. Barnett held the door open.

"Yes," she answered, "but at least he didn't get to the woods behind my house."

Eagerly they helped Mrs. Barnett spread the newspaper from the previous afternoon across the kitchen table.

"Look," said Drake, pointing to the article about the manhunt, "he is wanted in Harris County on suspicion of murder and credit card abuse. He is also charged with two counts of attempted murder in Denton County."

"Those last charges must have been filed

after he almost hit two officers at the rest stop before coming out here," said Mrs. Barnett.

"I'm glad he was captured," Amy stated.

"Yeah," Henry broke in, "the fire ants got him."

"Those ants are awesome," Drake added.

"I could have told you that," said Horace, smiling at Mrs. Barnett.

"Hey, where's Bo?" Drake inquired, as his eyes scanned the kitchen.

"In our excitement, I guess you didn't notice Bo was in the new dog pen I had built for him," Mrs. Barnett told them.

"That's a splendid idea," Amy responded. "Now, you can pen him up every afternoon before the newspaper comes."

"Yes," Mrs. Barnett answered, folding up the paper before setting out a plate of cookies. "It should be here in a minute, and we can read about my interview with the reporter."

They drank milk and ate chocolate chip cookies before going outside to get the newspaper.

When they did, Henry exclaimed, "There are two of them here!" Bo ran across the lawn bringing another one.

"I thought he was in his pen," chimed in Drake.

They walked around the corner of the house and found the gate open.

"How'd he do that?" Amy inquired.

"He must have lifted the latch with his paw," Horace replied.

"Let's sit on the porch while he brings the newspapers," Mrs. Barnett suggested.

Bo continued his task of depositing a newspaper on the porch and running to get another one. They took him to his pen after he finished.

"There's a hole at the bottom of the latch," Henry said, inspecting the gate. "If you put a stick through it, that should keep him inside."

"I'll put a lock through it," she smiled, settling on a stick for the time being.

Mrs. Barnett returned home from delivering the newspapers and let Bo out of his new pen. The evening air was chilly. She entered the house, and decided to have a cup of orange spice tea. After making her tea, she let it cool as she read the paper.

"Murder Suspect Loose in County," the headline read.

The article said residents were cautioned to stay inside and roads were closed while more than 35 law enforcement officers used search dogs and helicopters to hunt for the fugitive in a 4-square -mile area. It quoted Mrs. Barnett as saying deputies arrived at her door at 6:30 a.m. to warn her to stay inside.

"Helicopters and barking dogs could be heard between her home and the woods behind her house as neighbors continuously called each other to check their safety."

It pleased her that the article told how her neighbors looked out for one another. The telephone rang, interrupting her thoughts. It was Vandi Brown asking her to find a partner for her Saturday morning duty at the school's parking lot for Pride Day Clean-Up. Mrs. Barnett placed a call to Lorie Cooper, who at one time had been her teaching assistant.

"My car is in the shop, but I'll ask my daughter to bring me," Lorie said. "Can we pick you up?"

"No, but thank you. I am going to walk my son's dog to the school," she answered, thinking Bo would need more exercise now that he was to stay in a pen most of the time.

The next afternoon only three of the teenagers showed up at the door.

"It seems weird not having Bo to meet us," Amy said, as they entered the kitchen.

"I have him locked in his pen and also had a metal dog house delivered. We put it inside with him. Where is Henry?"

"I don't know," said Drake, shrugging his shoulders. "He wasn't at school today."

"I hope he isn't ill. How about some oatmeal cookies?" she invited.

The three of them sat down at the table, and after having a few cookies, they heard Bo bark.

"Oh, no," said Horace, jumping up from the table and heading for the door. "That bark came from the front yard."

He yanked open the door and all of them gazed out as Bo deposited a newspaper on the porch and ran off for another one.

"How'd he get out?" Amy asked, leaving the porch with the rest of them.

They hurried to the dog pen and found the gate locked.

"He must have jumped it," said Drake, "and I see how he did."

"Yes," Horace agreed, "he jumped on the roof of the dog house and sailed over the fence."

"The house gave him a boost," Mrs. Barnett despaired. "I might as well leave him out while I decide what to do."

"We'll help you return the newspapers until you do," Amy said, patting Mrs. Barnett's shoulder, trying to comfort her.

They waited for Bo to complete his undertaking and then returned the newspapers.

Mrs. Barnett entered the house. After dialing a number, she clutched the telephone to her ear.

"Your dog pulls up latches and jumps fences. . . . I can't keep him in anything. . . . What do you mean he loves me? . . .If that's the case, I don't want to think what he'd do if he hated me. . . . I enrolled him in a dog training class, but it doesn't begin until next month. . . . What has he done? . . . I'm still delivering newspapers! . . . You leave my legs out of it. . . . They're strong enough, thank you. . . . When are you coming home? . . . All right, I'll hold that thought – 'Bo will soon be a disciplined, obedient animal.'"

Chapter 10

The Stolen VCR

Saturday morning Mrs. Barnett hooked the leash to Bo's collar. He bounced on his front paws and barked excitedly, waiting for her to open the door. Once outside he stayed close to her side, and it surprised her to see how calm he had become. Turning on the shoulder of Old Justin Road, Mrs. Barnett felt rather pleased the way Bo was acting. She thought he showed a certain amount of dignity marching beside her, holding his head high. He continued in this fashion until he saw a neighborhood dog. Quickening his pace, he forced Mrs. Barnett to jog along behind him.

"Stop!" she commanded, which he did, but only after the other dog joined them. The two pawed each other, wagged their tails, and jumped in the air.

"Is this one of your friends?" Mrs. Barnett puffed, struggling with the leash.

She pulled and jerked until she managed to get Bo under control. They continued walking. The neighborhood dog followed. Soon the two dogs resumed their romping. They seemed to relish jumping in the air, falling down, and rolling on the ground. Mrs. Barnett nearly stumbled trying to step over them. Pulling hard on the leash, she forced Bo to straighten up, and he did for a while, until two more dogs joined them.

The four then pawed each other, jumped around, and rolled on the ground. Frequently they picked themselves up and ran in a pack. One minute, Mrs. Barnett pulled Bo. Next, he pulled her. He frolicked and raced all the way to the school's parking lot.

Lorie, wearing a denim dress and sneakers, stood watching as Mrs. Barnett ran across the bridge holding Bo's leash, following four dogs. She rushed to her. Mrs. Barnett ran past her, tossing the leash. Lorie grabbed it and took off running toward the administration building yelling all the commands necessary to stop a runaway, including, "HALT!"

Mrs. Barnett ran past her, tossing the leash.

With Bo in the lead, Lorie circled the building before shouting, "SIT!"

Bo directed her to Mrs. Barnett resting on the curb and sat down next to her. Lorie dropped the leash in Mrs. Barnett's hand and sank beside them.

"You . . . have . . . a . . . strong . . . dog," she gasped.

"I've experienced his strength," Mrs. Barnett answered, surprised that she was now breathing normally.

"I . . . think . . . my arms . . . got longer," Lorie said, stretching one out.

"Mine, too."

Both women sat quietly, until Lorie asked, "Did you know there is a bake sale in the cafeteria?"

"Yes, I brought oatmeal cookies last night. The Argyle Pride Task Force is raising money to build a walking and jogging path back there behind the school," she said, pointing.

They were looking in that direction when Mrs. Barnett caught a glimpse of someone, carrying a large object, walking across the pasture south of the school. At the same time a car pulled up to the trash bins. "We better get over there," Lorie suggested.

"I'll be there in a minute," Mrs. Barnett answered, standing up and straining to see if she recognized the person walking across the pasture. "It's Henry," she told herself.

She watched as he came closer. He stopped and appeared to look in her direction. She waved at the same time Bo perked up his ears and gave a soft cry. Straining forward, Bo began to bark loudly as he lunged ahead, running toward the pasture pulling Mrs. Barnett with him.

Henry put the object he was carrying down and ran back across the meadow. Bo slipped under the fence and stopped by a VCR lying on the ground.

Whining and sniffing, Bo ignored Mrs. Barnett's calls. In desperation she pulled the leash to her as hard as she could, prompting Bo to crawl back under the fence. With Bo following, Mrs. Barnett hurried to the administration building to find a telephone. She hadn't gone far before a police car drove up. It was Chief Partin.

"How is the clean-up day going?" he asked, driving up beside her.

"I guess it's doing all right," she answered, "but I was about to call you."

She told him about finding the VCR that Henry had carried across the pasture. Chief Partin got out of his car and walked with Mrs. Barnett and Bo as they showed him the way.

After climbing over the fence, he cautiously pulled back the grass from around the VCR. "What do we have here?"

"What?" Mrs. Barnett asked, anxiously, standing on the other side of the fence with Bo.

"The Hill's name is etched on it. What can you tell me about this boy?" he asked, crawling back over the fence.

While walking to the car, Mrs. Barnett told the police chief all she knew.

"I can't believe he is responsible for doing this," Mrs. Barnett said, "but there is something that has bothered me."

"What's that?" he asked, taking a pair of rubber gloves from the car seat and putting them on.

"During the burglary, the Hill's newspaper from the day before was taken."

"That's right," he agreed. "We thought they might have used it to put under some of the equipment they took."

She nodded in agreement. "After using it someone could have read it. In that edition there was a letter to the editor that was the only story printed about the Argyle Angel Tree. Two days after the Hill's house was burglarized, Henry told me his uncle hadn't started taking the newspaper, and he would like to have one to read more about the Angel Tree."

"He could have heard about it at school," Chief Partin offered as they walked back to the pasture.

"That's true, but the day he asked about it was his first day of school. His high school includes students from towns other than Argyle which makes me wonder why announcements would be made about our Angel Tree. Besides, he said he wanted to read more about it."

"It is curious," he said, picking up the VCR and putting it between the fence wire to the other side as he gently laid it on the ground before climbing over himself.

"Henry must have brought the VCR over to put in the trash," Mrs. Barnett said, shaking her head as she and Bo walked him back to the police car.

"Yes," he said. "It's a marked item."

Chief Partin said he would call her after he made some inquiries and drove off.

Mrs. Barnett and Bo joined Lorie who had set aside six pieces of discarded furniture that were in good enough condition for the garage sale.

"You have done rather well," Mrs. Barnett commended.

"Yes," Lorie beamed. "What have you been doing?"

"I can't talk about it since nothing is definite, but we did find a VCR over there with the Hill's name etched on it."

"Oh," said Lorie, "then the burglar must be from here?"

"I don't know. Say, it's about time for the next group to relieve us. Johnny Beavers volunteered to pick up the items we've kept for the sale and store them in our garages," Mrs. Barnett informed her.

"That's where garage sale stuff should be kept," Lorie laughed before quickly changing the subject. "Are you walking home with that dog?"

"We came together, and we're leaving together," Mrs. Barnett said with determination.

The walk home began uneventfully except for the neighborhood dog that followed. Nearing Henry's house, she saw a police car parked at the side. As she got closer, she watched Chief Partin escort Henry to the car. Bo whined and charged ahead. Mrs. Barnett ran behind him, but the car drove off before they reached it. Bo eagerly sniffed the lawn as Mrs. Barnett pulled on the leash and commanded him to leave. Eventually he stopped resisting and walked home the way he had left, holding his head high, staying close to Mrs. Barnett's side.

Monday morning Chief Partin called Mrs. Barnett to tell her he had taken Henry to the juvenile detention center on probable cause. He told her that he had no other alternative since Henry refused to talk.

"He wouldn't answer any of your questions about the VCR?" Mrs. Barnett inquired.

"All he would say was that he found it, and when I asked him where, he said he didn't know. He doesn't know where he read about the Argyle Angel Tree or where he got the newspaper that told about it. You saw him carrying the VCR, and his fingerprints are the only ones on it, but he still doesn't know where he got it."

"Was Henry's thumbprint the one found at the Hill's house?" she inquired.

"No, it wasn't. It was a man named Davenport Smith, alias, Bob Couch, and alias, Seat Morgan."

"You're kidding."

"No, I'm not," he laughed. "The man has a long record of thefts from all over the country, and we are still in the process of checking on him."

"How did Henry get involved with him!" she exclaimed.

"Henry doesn't know," came the reply.

"Where is he now?" she asked.

"He's at home. His uncle picked him up from the detention center Saturday, but he will be going before the judge this afternoon."

"I still don't think Henry burglarized the Hill's house."

"I hope you're right," he said, ending the conversation.

Chapter 11

A Visit to Henry's Uncle

Monday afternoon Drake, Horace, and Amy rushed to Mrs. Barnett's porch to tell her what they had heard about Henry.

"Chief Partin told me," she said, inviting them inside.

Bo stretched out on the floor beside the kitchen table where the teenagers took seats. Mrs. Barnett sat down and began telling them how she and Bo found the VCR.

"If Bo could talk, he would have told Chief Partin that Henry took the VCR to the pasture. Bo can smell anything Henry touches," Horace said.

"Yes, I've seen him find a stick that Henry has thrown when it lands in a bunch of them," Amy declared.

"I still don't think he did it," Drake stated, crossing his arms over his chest and shaking his head.

"I know you're upset," Mrs. Barnett said sympathetically. "But Henry is in trouble because he would not answer the questions the authorities asked him. If he says, 'I don't know,' to the judge this afternoon, he's in bigger trouble."

"He certainly is," Amy declared, "but I don't think he's guilty either."

Mrs. Barnett set out a plate of peanut butter cookies while Amy and Horace filled their glasses with milk.

"Let's try to figure out what happened," volunteered Horace, taking a cookie from the plate. "Now somewhere Henry got the same edition of the newspaper the burglars took from the Hill's house because he knew about the Angel Tree, and somewhere he got the Hill's VCR because their name was on it. Oh, that doesn't look good."

"He could be covering up for his uncle," suggested Mrs. Barnett.

"And that would be why he isn't saying

anything," Drake said enthusiastically as he began eating a cookie.

"Chief Partin said he would call me after the hearing," Mrs. Barnett told them. "In the meantime, I have something to show you."

After they finished their snacks, they followed Bo and Mrs. Barnett outside. "I brought these up from the rock garden and had to use the wheel barrow to haul that big one," she said, pointing to a large, white fossil.

"These look like huge snails," said Amy.

"That's what they are, Amy," Drake answered, bending over to get a closer look.

"How old are they?" Horace asked, turning over one of the spiral, shelled fossils.

"They are about 200 million years old or older," Mrs. Barnett informed them.

"Oh," voiced Amy, rather surprised. "Do you have more?"

"No, but when Henry . . ."

They heard the telephone ringing. Drake hurried inside to answer it before the party hung up.

"It's the police chief," he said, handing the receiver to Mrs. Barnett when she entered the room.

"Yes, Chief Partin," she answered.

She nodded through most of the conversation while her guests stood by whispering, "What?"

Mrs. Barnett then asked if she could talk to Henry. "I certainly will," she said. "Thank you so much for calling."

Turning to the three youngsters she said, "I was afraid Henry wouldn't answer the judge's questions and he didn't. Therefore, he is to stay at the juvenile detention center indefinitely."

"Can you talk to him?" Amy asked.

"Yes, I'm going to in the morning. Where is Bo?"

They stepped outside and found two rolled up newspapers lying on the porch.

"Did you really need to ask?" Drake laughed.

They waited for Bo to finish his newspaper snatching. Then they returned them.

The next morning, Mrs. Barnett dressed and closed Bo inside the kitchen. She stopped at Henry's house before going to the juvenile detention center. His uncle was at home and answered the door.

"I'm Mrs. Barnett, a neighbor, and I'm very fond of your nephew. Could I speak with you?" she asked.

"I've heard a lot about you and your dog, Bo," he answered, inviting her inside.

"He's not my dog, but we won't go into that. I'm going to the center to visit Henry, and I wondered if you could tell me why he won't tell the judge where he found the VCR?"

"I have no idea," came his reply.

He told her the police chief had left only a few minutes before and asked him the same question.

"The day of the burglary Henry and I were together most of the time. We were right here unpacking. Then I went to town to do some bank business and left Henry to finish," he told her.

"Do you know a Davenport Smith, a Bob Couch, or a Seat Morgan?"

"No, I don't, and the police chief asked me that same question. I am so worried about Henry," he said, showing genuine concern. "The idea of his being locked up is awful."

"What about your friends who helped you move in?" she questioned.

"As I told you, I don't know anybody by those names."

Mrs. Barnett thanked him for his time and left promising to do what she could for Henry. On her way she stopped by the Argyle Police Department. Finding Chief Partin she said, "I am on my way to see Henry, but before I do, I would like to talk to you."

"Sure," he said, in his friendly manner.

She told him she thought Henry might not be answering questions because he wanted to protect his uncle. Chief Partin agreed that could be a possibility but assured her he had checked the uncle's account of what he did the day of the burglary. "If he was with Henry at the times he said he was, his uncle was not involved."

"That's all I wanted to hear," Mrs. Barnett grinned, thanking him as she left.

Chapter 12

Visiting the Detention Center

Driving into the parking lot of the Denton County Juvenile Detention Center, Mrs. Barnett parked the car and went inside. She told the deputy whom she wanted to see. Before going to the waiting room she went through a metal detector, and a deputy looked though her purse. Mrs. Barnett looked at the boy as the officer escorted him into the room. Henry's tall form looked gaunt, and his face showed signs of sadness.

"Henry, I am so sorry all of this is happening to you," Mrs. Barnett said.

"How is Bo?" he asked, trying to smile.

"I think he misses you. I know I do, and I want you to come home," she said. "Henry, I think you are trying to keep your uncle out of trouble for something you think he might have done. Will you tell me where you found the VCR?"

"I don't want to cause problems for my uncle," he replied.

"That's what I thought. I talked to your uncle before coming here, and I also talked to Chief Partin," she informed him, as she continued. "Your uncle said he was with you or at the bank the day of the burglary. He was with you before 11 a.m. and after 1 p.m., was he not?"

"Yes," Henry answered.

"Well, there you are. Chief Partin has witnesses and a bank deposit slip stating he was at the bank when he said he was. Also the thumbprint found at the Hill's house isn't yours or your uncle's."

"The police found a thumbprint at the Hill's house?" he inquired.

"Yes, and they need you to answer their questions to help them catch the burglar."

"So my uncle wasn't involved!" Henry exclaimed, brightening up.

"No," she answered. "Now, where did you

get the VCR, and where did you get the newspaper that told about the Angel Tree?"

"I guess it was the day after the burglary. I found the newspaper on the floor under a box. It was open to the editorial page and I read it."

"The newspaper must have been carried in with the boxes," Mrs. Barnett pondered. "Who brought those boxes in the house?"

"I don't remember. My uncle's buddies helped us sometimes, but I don't remember exactly when."

"What are his buddies names?"

"Funny nicknames-one is 'Cash' Mixon and the other one is 'Frenchy' Settee. We met them in Arkansas, and my uncle considered going into business with them, but decided not to and started his rock business. 'Cash' and 'Frenchy' look for fast ways to get money. They only come by once in a while, and I don't know where they live."

"Henry, I'm going to see if I can get you another hearing before the judge," she said hastily. "First, you need to tell me where you got the VCR."

"I found it in the back of my uncle's truck the morning I didn't go to school. I stayed home to see if anyone would pick it up or if my uncle would take it off, but nothing happened. I saw the Hill's name on it, and on the Pride Day Clean-up I tried to take the VCR to a trash bin, but you know the rest."

Mrs. Barnett called Chief Partin. She told him Henry would answer all of his questions. "Now that he knows his uncle won't be implicated, he's willing to tell you all he knows."

The police chief said he would talk to the district attorney about scheduling another hearing. Mrs. Barnett then contacted Henry's uncle and suggested he come to the detention center.

"I'll be right there," he said, sounding greatly relieved.

Mrs. Barnett returned to Henry.

"Chief Partin is in the process of arranging another hearing, and your uncle is coming to be with you," she told him. "Henry, if you need anything, please call me."

"I will, Mrs. Barnett, and thank you," he smiled.

Chapter 13

The Capture

That afternoon the three teenagers ran up Mrs. Barnett's steps to her porch. "What happened at the jail today?" Drake asked Mrs. Barnett as she held the door open.

"Drake, it's a juvenile detention center," Amy corrected, walking into the house.

"It's the same thing. They're only divided by age," he informed her.

"For some reason juvenile detention center sounds better," she responded. "Yes, do tell us what happened."

Mrs. Barnett told them how Henry had thought his uncle might be a suspect in the burglary if he said anything, but when he found out he wasn't involved, he started talking. Her guests listened intently as she told them where Henry found the VCR and the newspaper that told about the Angel Tree.

She began telling them the names of his uncle's friends when Bo started barking and running to the door.

"Newspaper time!" Horace exclaimed, letting Bo outside.

Quickly Mrs. Barnett set out a plate of snickerdoodles.

"I almost forgot to put these on the table," she said, getting glasses from the cabinet.

"I really like this kind of cookie," Drake said, pouring everyone a glass of juice before taking one.

They ate cookies and drank a juice punch while Bo ran to pick up newspapers. After he completed his task, they led him to his pen and started returning them.

"I hope Henry comes home soon," said Horace as they finished delivering their last one.

"I hope so too," Mrs. Barnett said, waving goodbye.

She let Bo out of the pen and went into the

house to read the afternoon paper while he went for a run. Suddenly there was loud banging at the door with Henry shouting, "Mrs. Barnett! Mrs. Barnett!"

She jumped up and hurried to answer it. "Henry, when did you get home?"

"Not very long ago, but will you call Chief Partin?"

"Yes," she answered, hurrying to the telephone.

"Tell him," he said breathlessly, "my uncle's friends are at my house now . . .and. . .and. . . I remember on the day of the burglary they were there early in the morning. Then they left but returned later to help us bring in the rest of the boxes. Tonight 'Cash' asked me to get him a flashlight out of the glove compartment. I opened the truck door and lying on the seat was a pair of leather gloves. I accidentally knocked them off getting the flashlight, and when I picked them up, I saw the thumb of one of the gloves had a big hole in it."

"That would leave a thumbprint," Mrs. Barnett gasped. "What did you do with them?"

"I smoothed them out and laid them on the seat."

As she dialed the Argyle Police Department, she asked him, "Do they know you are gone?"

"Yes, I told them that when I saw you today, you asked me to come by and pick up some cookies you baked for my uncle and me. I didn't know what else to tell them so I could get away to call Chief Partin."

"That was smart . . .Hello, Chief Partin. Henry is here, and you need to know what he's found out."

Henry leaned over and whispered, "Tell him I'll be at my house."

"Just a minute, Chief Partin," she said, turning to Henry.

"Henry, grab a bunch of cookies out of the cookie jar and take Bo with you. Tell them you're taking him for a walk."

"I'm here," she said into the telephone. "Henry is going back home so that his uncle's friends won't suspect anything and leave."

Quickly she told him how Henry had found

a glove with part of the thumb missing, and how he now remembered that his uncle's friends had helped them move in on the day of the burglary, putting the men only doors away from the Hill's house.

They ended the conversation with Chief Partin saying he was on his way. Mrs. Barnett rushed to her car and drove down Old Justin Road to Henry's house. Stopping on the other side of the street a short distance from where he lived, she watched as Chief Partin approached the old, blue pick-up truck with two men inside. The door was open on the driver's side, and Chief Partin stood in front of it. Mrs. Barnett rolled down the window, but what they were saying was not loud enough for her to hear. Chief Partin seemed to be doing the talking.

"That must be 'Frenchy,'" she thought, watching the man in the driver's seat smile and shake his head.

Chief Partin took the police radio off his belt, and as he talked on it, he turned his head away from the men in the truck. 'Frenchy' and his companion appeared to be fumbling with something in the seat. They seemed unsure as to what to do. Finally 'Frenchy' moved forward putting it behind him. Chief Partin, unaware of this scheme, took his position at the door. As he talked, 'Frenchy' smiled and shook his head. Henry and Bo, standing at a distance, walked closer. Suddenly Henry pointed to the truck and yelled, "Fetch."

Frantically, Bo smelled the ground. Sticking his head inside the truck, he sniffed the floor board. 'Frenchy' moved over as Bo ran his nose along the edge of the seat. Catching the scent, Bo rammed his head behind the driver, pinning 'Frenchy' against the steering wheel. Poking and shoving, he searched behind him. All at once the hunt was over, and Bo carried his discovery to Henry.

"Good dog," Henry shouted, removing a pair of gloves from dog's mouth and handing them to Chief Partin.

Chief Partin examined them and said loudly, "That's what we need, Henry."

With his head slumped forward, 'Frenchy' slowly got out of the truck. Chief Partin handcuffed him and led him to the police car.

All at once the hunt was over.

Frenchy's' companion started the engine of their truck and drove off.

Leaving her car, Mrs. Barnett walked over to Henry and Bo who were glad to see her. Henry hugged her and Bo strutted around with a stick in his mouth. Henry's uncle came out of the house saying he watched from the window with one hand on the telephone in case there was an emergency. They patted each other on the shoulder and gave high five's.

A photographer from the newspaper came to take pictures of Henry and Bo before Mrs. Barnett left. He had heard on his police scanner how they assisted in capturing the burglar.

The next afternoon the four teenagers raced to Mrs. Barnett's porch. "Come in. I have a surprise for all of you," she said, opening the door.

Party decorations spread throughout the kitchen. Brightly colored balloons with long streamers bounced around the ceiling. Beautiful cakes, trays of cookies, and glasses filled with a colorful punch sat on the table. Bo wore a pointed party hat that in the excitement began slipping over his eyes.

"Everything is so pretty!" Amy exclaimed, showing her excitement. The boys nodded, looking around and letting their eyes take it all in. Henry bent over to adjust Bo's hat.

"It's time to celebrate," Mrs. Barnett announced ushering her guests to the table.

As they ate chocolate cake with walnuts, carrot cake with cream cheese icing, and drank punch, they talked about the events that lead to the capture of 'Frenchy.' Abruptly Bo interrupted their conversation, barking and running to the door. Drake pulled off the dog's hat before letting him outside and went outside himself to bring in the afternoon paper.

"Here it is," he said, moving plates to spread the newspaper across the table.

"That is such a good picture of you and Bo, Henry," Amy commented.

"When did 'Frenchy' put the VCR in the back of your uncle's pickup?" Horace questioned.

"Perhaps the night before I found it. He must have seen the Hill's name on it and decided to frame my uncle. I don't know, but it will probably come out in the trial."

"Was his buddy 'Cash' in on it?" Drake asked.

"Yes, the police now have him in custody after he tried to dispose of the Hill's property," Henry said, reaching for a cookie.

"Well," said Mrs. Barnett, "let's see if Bo has finished bringing us the newspapers."

Bo was lying on the porch waiting for them. They took him to his pen and returned the papers.

After Mrs. Barnett let Bo out for a run, she went into the house and walked over to the telephone.

"This is your mother, and your dog is a hero. . . . I will send you the newspaper clippings that tells all about it. . . . No, he is still your dog. . . .When are you coming home?. . . . Can we discuss your job later? I am rather tired. . . .Yes, I'll call you soon."

Chapter 14

The Famous Retriever

The following evening after returning the newspapers, she heard the telephone ringing when she entered the house. It was Pat. She was writing another letter to the newspaper and needed Mrs. Barnett's up-to-date senior citizen's report, "'Right now. Tonight!"

Delighted with all the gifts the Argyle Angel Tree had received, Mrs. Barnett didn't want to delay Pat's letter to the editor. Hurriedly she brushed her short, wavy hair and put on a coat. As she rushed out the door, Bo ran to her with a stick in his mouth.

"Not now," she told him, shoving him aside. He followed her to the car and as she tried to slide under the steering wheel he put his paws in her lap.

"Oh Bo," she said, petting his head as he struggled to get in with her. "You have been a good dog, and you did capture a burglar, but I need to leave."

She pushed him out the door and quickly closed it yelling, "SIT!"

She drove off, but Bo followed. She backed the car up to the house, rolled down the window, and shouted, "SIT!"

He did, but only as long as the car wasn't moving. "All right!" she shouted, slamming on the brakes and bending over to open the door on the passenger's side. Bo charged in and sat down.

Leaning across him to close the door, Bo licked her cheek. A smile crossed her lips thinking about what a hero he had become.

"Sharing this new experience of riding in the car together is nice," she thought, feeling a special fondness for her slick, black companion.

Bo seemed contented sitting beside her in the front seat, looking out the windshield. When she parked the car at Pat's house she yelled, "SIT," but Bo tried to get out with her. She managed to close the door before he could.

Pat invited her inside and feeling more relaxed than she had on her previous visit, Mrs. Barnett accepted. Once inside she explained the report to Pat as they enjoyed a cup of hot tea and Scottish shortbread fingers. Mrs. Barnett declined a second cup of tea stating she needed to leave, and after saying goodbye, she walked to her car.

The dome light came on when she opened the door, and she found Bo sitting in the driver's seat. Immediately her eyes raced through the inside of the car and she reeled in disbelief, momentarily thinking, "Someone's stolen my car and left me with this pile of junk!"

Puffs of foam rubber blew out the door as Bo bounced on the front seat. Hoping no one could see her jolting predicament hurriedly she jumped under the steering wheel and promptly sank to the floor. Closing the door, she noticed the vinyl stripped from it. Reaching for the seat belt, she found it chewed into pieces. The headrest was a metal stub, and the sun visor had vinyl streamers dangling from it. The black dog immediately wrapped his front legs around her shoulders and affectionately drooled saliva down her cheek. As she strained to see over the dash-

She found Bo sitting in the driver's seat.

board, her son's words flashed through her mind, "Talk to him."

"The words I have for you, you wouldn't want to hear," she seethed, nudging the dog's chest with her elbow trying to get him to move over.

Upon arriving home, she ran to the telephone. ". . . But son, my car. No seat, no headrest, no door panel, no seat belt, no sun visor . . . What do you mean you're glad we're so close, and he just wanted to stay with me? . . . Yes, I'll send you the bill."

The next day, Mrs. Barnett threw a blanket over the front seat and drove into town. When she explained her problem to the auto upholster, he asked to see the car. She made him promise not to laugh, but when she uncovered the front seat, his muted snickers exploded into loud laughter.

"It's not funny," she said despairingly.

"I know," the man sputtered, "but that dog sure must have had the munchies."

Upon her return home, she called her son . . . "Yes, the car is in the shop, and two men brought me home because they wanted to see the dog that likes to eat vinyl. When are you coming home? . . . Yes, I'm sitting down. . . . What? . . . Not for two years, but maybe for visits, you say! . . .What do you mean Bo will take care of me? He hasn't so far. He's chewed or eaten anything he can get his teeth into. My next door neighbors think I'm hard of hearing, shouting those commands for him to sit and stay; I return six newspapers every evening; I bake cookies for the little kid down the street to make up for his sand bucket; and I'm the laughing stock of the upholstery shop. . . . Yes, I'll empty your closets and box up everything. . . . Yes, you're right. I shouldn't get lonesome. . . . Yes, I have Bo scheduled for a dog training class. . . . I'm glad you like your job, son."

She put down the receiver and let the black dog into the kitchen. He stood beside her as she gently patted his head.

"It's just you and me," she whispered, blinking back tears as she looked down at the dog. "I guess we can live together. At least, you're house broken and don't talk back."

The black dog nudged her leg with his nose. She knelt down beside him, cradling his moist jaws into her hands, and said softly, "I think he knew he wasn't coming back home the day he brought me 'the famous retriever.'"

The End